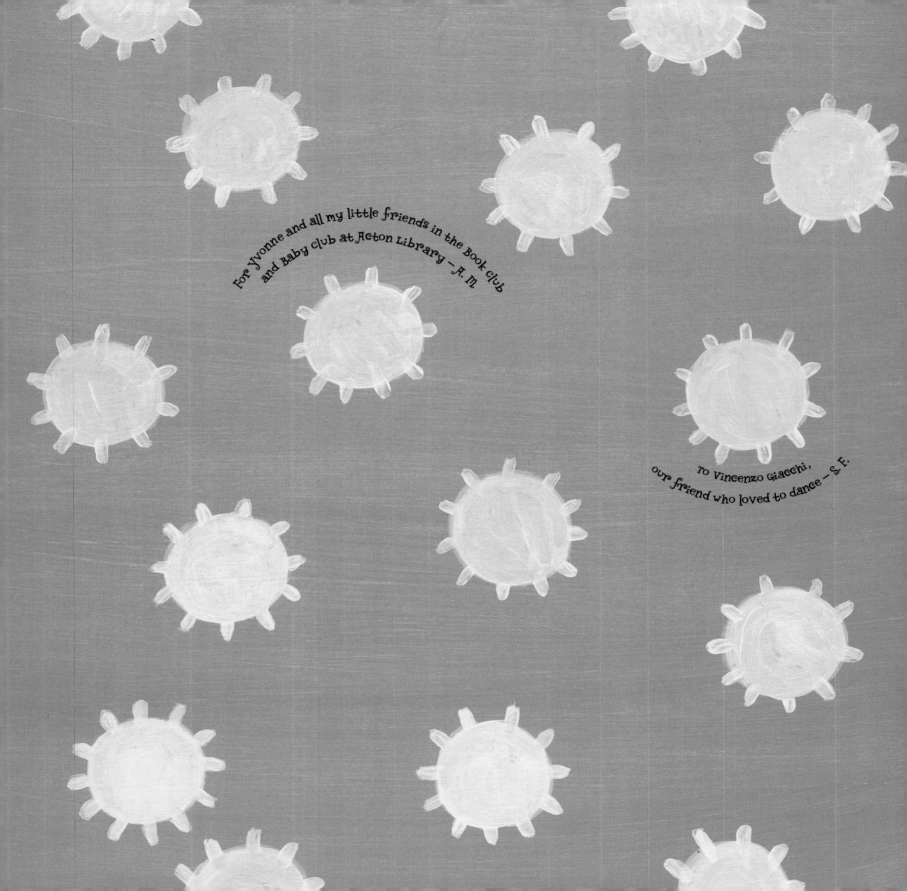

For Yvonne and all my little friends in the Book club
and Baby club at Acton Library – A. M.

To Vincenzo Giacchi,
our friend who loved to dance – S. F.

If You're Happy and You Know it!

adapted by Anna McQuinn

illustrated by Sophie Fatus

Barefoot Books
Celebrating Art and Story

If you're happy and you know it, clap your hands!
If you're happy and you know it, clap your hands!
If you're happy and you know it,
and you really want to show it,
If you're happy and you know it,
clap your hands!

If you're happy and you know it,
and you really want to show it,

If you're happy and you know it,
stamp your feet!
If you're happy and
you know it, stamp your feet!

If you're happy and you know it,
stamp your feet!

If you're happy and you know it, turn around!
If you're happy and you know it, turn around!
If you're happy and you know it, and you really want to show it,
If you're happy and you know it, turn around!

If you're happy and you know it, wiggle your hips!
If you're happy and you know it, wiggle your hips!
If you're happy and you know it, and you really want to show it,
If you're happy and you know it, wiggle your hips!

If you're happy and you know it, stretch your arms!
If you're happy and you know it, stretch your arms!
If you're happy and you know it, and you really want to show it,

If you're happy and you know it, stretch your arms!

If you're happy and you know it, pat your head!
If you're happy and you know it, pat your head!
If you're happy and you know it, and you really want to show it,
If you're happy and you know it, Pat your head!

If you're happy and you know it, touch your nose!
If you're happy and you know it, touch your nose!
If you're happy and you know it, and you really want to show it,
If you're happy and you know it, touch your nose!

If you're happy and you know it, point your toes!
If you're happy and you know it, point your toes!
If you're happy and you know it, and you really want to show it,
If you're happy and you know it, point your toes!

If you're happy and you know it, shout hello!
If you're happy and you know it, shout hello!
If you're happy and you know it, and you really want to show it,
If you're happy and you know it, shout hello!

Aurélie
France

Ming Hoa
China (Mandarin)

Lulu
Tanzania

Omar
Pakistan

Konrad
Poland

Simran
India (Hindi)

Fetsum
Ethiopia

Fatima
Malaysia

Sukhinder
India (Punjabi)

Sasha
Russia

Annette
Austria

Oisín
Ireland

Arina
Afghanistan

Shota
N. America (Lak...

Zainab
Lebanon

Calida
Greece

Pedro
Portugal

Bente
The Netherlan...

Himari
Japan

Vittorio
Italy

Robindra
Bangladesh

Muna
Somalia

Jubulani
Zimbabwe

Sōng
China   (Cantonese)

Raúl
Spain

Nkem
Nigeria

Kajarithan
Sri Lanka

Yeab
Eritrea

Hanne
Germany

Mehmet
Turkey

Ben
Canada

Yasbet
Mexico

Saimi
Finland

Arapoosh
N. America (Apsaaloke)

Shane
Australia

Kirima
Canada (Inukitut)

If You're Happy and You Know it

If you're hap — py and you know it clap your hands! If you're

hap — py and you know it clap your hands! If you're hap — py and you know it, and you

real — ly want to show it, if you're hap—py and you know it, clap your hands!

To add words to this song from each of
the languages featured in this book,
please search for **If You're Happy and You Know It**
at www.barefootbooks.com

Barefoot Books
2067 Massachusetts Ave
Cambridge, MA 02140

Barefoot Books
124 Walcot Street
Bath, BA1 5BG

Music arranged and composed by Susan Reed, www.susanreed.com
Performed by Susan Reed, Kate Reed and Allison Reed
Recorded, mixed and mastered by Eric Kilburn at Wellspring Sound, Acton, MA

First published in Great Britain by Barefoot Books Ltd
and in the United States of America by Barefoot Books Inc in 2009
Graphic design by Louise Millar, London. Reproduction by Grafiscan, Verona
Printed and bound on 100% acid-free paper in China by Printplus Ltd
This book was typeset in Neu Phollick Alpha & Circus Dog
The illustrations were prepared in acrylics

ISBN 978-1-84686-288-5

Library of Congress Cataloging-in-Publication Data is available under LCCN 2008039827
British Cataloguing-in-Publication Data:
a catalogue record for this book is available from the British Library

1 3 5 7 9 8 6 4 2

Barefoot Books
Celebrating Art and Story

At Barefoot Books, we celebrate art and story that opens
the hearts and minds of children from all walks of life, inspiring
them to read deeper, search further, and explore their own creative gifts.
Taking our inspiration from many different cultures, we focus on themes that
encourage independence of spirit, enthusiasm for learning, and sharing of
the world's diversity. Interactive, playful and beautiful, our products
combine the best of the present with the best of the past to
educate our children as the caretakers of tomorrow.

Live Barefoot!

Join us at www.barefootbooks.com

Anna McQuinn trained as a teacher of children's literature, and has been working in children's publishing for over sixteen years as an editor, a publisher and writer. She also runs regular groups at a local library with movement, stories, singing and rhyme times for small children. She lives in Slough, England with her husband. This is her first project with Barefoot Books, and was inspired by the library groups she runs in London where children from all over the world come together to sing "If You're Happy and You Know It!".

Sophie Fatus is a full-time illustrator and sculptress who studied at the prestigious Academy of Fine Art in Paris. Her bright illustrations and quirky style are world-renowned and have graced the pages of many Barefoot books including *The Story Tree* (2001), *Babushka* (2002), *My Daddy is a Pretzel* (2004), *Yoga Pretzels* (2005), *Here We Go Round the Mulberry Bush* (2007) and *Yoga Planet* (2008). Sophie lives in Florence, Italy.